Desired

One Handed Reads
Book 5

Dee Lish

Chapter One

Five Months Later

I have to be honest; this isn't the situation I had in mind when I first hooked back up with Noah. I'm standing in the middle of my living room, and Daniel is going mental. Judgy Bitch is glaring at me with the mother of all 'I told you so' looks on her face as she watches everything unfolding from her high horse.

Noah is sitting there, calm, letting Daniel rant. Yes, you heard that correctly. Noah is in my living room too. My husband, my lover, and me, all in the same room at the same time. The fire and brimstone raining down on me right now would set the whole world alight.

"Dan, can you just calm down?" I plead.

He glares, and I swear it almost cuts right through my soul. He's distraught. He's incredibly angry, and given what he's just found out, I don't blame him. I feel guilty. I feel like an utter arsehole who has just shattered his happiness and my own. I wouldn't have wanted him to find out about my affair with Noah this way. Truth be told, I'm not sure I would ever have wanted him to find out.

"You're fucking someone else. You are having an affair. You're an adulterous fucking whore. What the fuck is there to be calm about, Gemma?" Daniel spits. "I mean, have I missed anything? You're getting on like a fucking slut, and I'm meant to be calm?"

I sigh and hang my head in defeat. "What do you want me to say?"

"I would say you should at least be sorry, but I already know that would be another lie."

I fight back the tears. I don't deserve to feel sorry for myself. He is right, though. As sorry as I am for the hurt I'm causing him, I'm not actually sorry for having the affair. For whatever kind of shitty person that makes me, I am sorry, but I can't lie; I don't regret seeing Noah even once.

"Is he better than me?" Daniel asks.

I blush. I never thought he would need to know, and that I would have to reassure him that it was always better with him. In my moment of hesitation, Dan grabs me. Noah stands, ready to pounce, and my husband glares at him, daring him to move.

"Why does one of us have to be better?" Noah asks.

"Don't you dare stand up for her!" I pull my wrist from his grasp while he's distracted. "Think you're the better man, do you? Well, let's just think about how that went when you had your fucking chance, shall we, dickhead? That's right. You pissed your opportunity to have her up the wall. You fucked off and never came back."

Noah's face falls and he looks at me. "I know."

"She's mine. You can't waltz back in here and take her. I married her. And don't fucking look at her, she's not for you. You lost her!" Daniel spins to look at me. "I'm not doing this, Gemma. I am your damn husband. I deserve better than this."

"I know you do." I know I should say sorry, but I still can't bring myself to say the words when I know I won't mean them. I've hurt him. I'm an adulterer. I'm a bitch. But I can't ever say I'm sorry for being with Noah.

Dan stares at me so intently; I can feel the scars marking my soul. "It's him or me, Gemma. You can't have us both."

"Daniel!" I plead. Judgy Bitch can be heard almost laughing, muttering something about making my bed and lying in it, and I can't think straight.

"What if she loves us both?" Noah interjects.

Daniel spins around with lightning speed, and I fear he's going to punch Noah. "Don't fucking push me, Redmond. You can't love two people at the same time."

"But what if she did? Why can't she have us both?"

I look at Noah like he's lost his ever-loving mind. I'm starting to wonder if he has a death wish, a sick sense of humour, perhaps. Something that is clearly making him not take in the emotions on a knife's edge within my husband.

"SHE'S MY FUCKING WIFE!" Dan screams at him.

Noah, surprisingly, keeps his cool. "She's a human being with her own thoughts and feelings. She's not a possession. You can't just piss on your territory and mark it as yours."

Oh, Jesus. This is going to end in carnage. I'm going to have to call for an ambulance and the police are going to come, and all fucking hell is going to break loose.

"Noah, leave it!" I want this to end. I can't watch this anymore. I can't watch Dan so hurt and know I caused it.

"Do you love me?" Daniel asks out of the blue, staring at me.

I don't even hesitate. I look at him, and the words

naturally fall from my lips. "Of course I do. With all my heart."

I look at Noah, his face sullen. "And do you love me, Gem?" he asks.

"Yes." I murmur the word out in the open before I even think.

A small hint of a smile creeps over Noah's face, and the irony isn't lost on me. I've just told him that I love him for the first time since all this started, in the middle of a battle that could end up with it being the last time.

Dread fills me at that thought. I can't. I can't lose either of them. But, God help me, Noah is right. I do love them both. I don't want to not have either of them in my life. I need them both.

"I love you both," I blurt. "I can't live without either of you. I wish I could pick one or the other, but I just can't."

Noah looks at me with a regretful smile. I know he hates that I'm being forced to confront all this. Daniel looks at me with incredulous disbelief. "What, so you think that I should fucking share you with him?"

I can't find the words to reply. I'm honestly not sure what the right answer is when your husband finds out that, not only have you been having an affair, but that you're actually in love with the person that you've been having the affair with, and want to keep being married AND shagging the other man. I flop to the sofa, exhausted. I just can't process everything right now. Three hours ago, I was in the post-orgasmic bliss with Noah between my thighs and now... now I'm in hell, and it's all of my own making.

"I don't know. Yes? Maybe... I... I just don't know."

Dan stares at me then Noah, and then turns to the door. "I can't fucking deal with this. I just can't..." he stutters.

Seconds later, he slams the front door and he's in the car and down the street. Gone.

"Could you really share me?" I ask, looking at Noah.

"If it was the only way of keeping you in my life? Fuck yes. I would rather that than be without you. I'm going to go. It's probably best I'm not here again when Daniel comes back." He leans over and kisses me softly. "And, I love you too," he tells me before heading for the door too.

The front door slams, and I watch through the window as Noah also disappears out of sight. I'm filled with a dread that this might just be my future from now on, without either of them. My eyes burn and tears start to fall. A sob chokes in my throat.

I have to find a way to make this work. My whole world, heart, and soul are wrapped up in those two beautiful men.

Chapter Two

I hear the front door open and I prepare myself for the next round in the battle with Dan. I haven't heard from him since he took off this afternoon after finding out what was happening with me and Noah.

I stand in the kitchen, my cold coffee cup in my hand, and I freeze. I don't know what to do. I don't know if I want to start the argument again. I don't know what Daniel is thinking. Judgy Bitch hasn't stopped nagging me all fucking day, and my eyes are red and sore from crying.

I hear him. I hear him hit his toe on the hall end table. "Fuck," he mumbles. He's drunk. I can't say I blame him. I'd probably head out and get shitfaced too in the circumstances. Just then, he turns the corner into the kitchen and sees me, stopping dead.

Pure hatred is coming off him in waves. *What do you expect?* Judgy Bitch reminds me.

"There she is, ladies and gentlemen. My adoring fucking wife," he jeers, his arms outstretched like he's addressing a crowd.

I sigh. *Round two, here you come!* sneers Judgy Bitch. Dan hears my exasperation and glares.

"Oh, I'm sorry, Mrs Elliott. Is the word of your adulterous whoring old news to you already?"

"You're drunk." I attempt to move past him.

He grabs me by the wrist and stops me in my tracks. "And you're a whore." He moves closer, invading my space. He's so close, I can smell the scotch on his breath. "A filthy fucking slut," he slurs.

I close my eyes and turn my face away. *Don't fucking cry,* Judgy Bitch warns. *You brought this all on yourself.*

"Is his dick bigger than mine, Gemma? Did he leave your pretty little cunt feeling well fucked afterwards?"

This time, I can't stop the tears from falling. "It's not about who's better or worse, it's just different," I answer honestly.

"Different?" He tightens his grip on my wrist and moves even more into my personal space. "Well, that makes it all okay that you're fucking him then, doesn't it? It's not because I leave you unsatisfied, it's just because you're a filthy cheating whore who fancied fucking someone *different.*"

Something in me snaps and I can't fight the urge to lash out. In a split-second, my hand comes up to Daniel's face, but before it can make contact, he grabs it. He pushes both hands behind my back, surrounding me, pressing himself against me. His mouth crushes against mine. There's a raw passion in it that hasn't been there for a while. He moves against me and I'm very aware of how turned on he is. It's not the traditional response of a husband who has just found out his wife is cheating on him.

His tongue is forcefully fucking my mouth, and I can't help myself; I lean into him and enjoy his fierce reaction.

He lets go of my wrists and grabs handfuls of my ass instead. I wrap my arms around his neck and bask in the unadulterated lust rolling off my husband.

"Dan," I moan when his lips leave mine and reach my neck instead.

Instantly, his hand covers my mouth. "Don't fucking speak to me yet," he sneers and sucks harder on the flesh on my neck. I already know what he's doing. He's marking me. He's being a horny teenage boy and leaving a love bite on my neck. Part of me wants to protest, to tell him that he can't do this to me; I have clients to see in the morning, and a love bite isn't exactly a professional look. But the other part of me is getting off on his reaction, is craving more, and needs him to keep going.

His hand moves from my mouth to my neck, cupping my face. His thumb directs me to move my head with a gentle pressure, allowing him better access. I willingly let him move me, basking in the lust-fuelled manhandling. This is the hottest reaction I've ever had from Daniel, and it's caught me totally off guard.

I gasp at the forcefulness of his mouth on my tender throat. I feel like a lamb exposed to a wolf. His anger and lust mix in a heady combination. I'm turned on, I want to know what's going to happen next, and despite everything, I want this to end up with my husband fucking me.

Dan pushes me back, moving step by step with me. My ass hits the kitchen counter. Daniel, again, presses himself against me. His lips find mine and he claims my mouth aggressively. I moan against him, every nerve I have on fire with a lust I've not felt with Daniel for years.

Daniel grinds against me, his cock rock hard against my lower stomach. I hunger to have him inside me. I don't want to ask him; I don't want to speak at all in case he changes his mind.

Getting off on this, are we? Judgy Bitch taunts, and, God, she's right. I am. I'm turned on by Daniel's jealousy. I'm turned on by his aggression. Something inside me is completely turned on by his reaction.

I risk touching him. My hand tentatively goes to his waist.

Daniel hisses, pries his lips from mine, and growls. "Don't fucking touch me." He grabs my hands and forces them behind me again. "Don't speak to me and don't touch me!" He seizes my mouth again.

I stand there, pressed against the countertop, doing as I'm told, taking what I'm given, enjoying every minute of it. I melt against him.

Daniel spins me around, my arse suddenly against his cock. He presses my hands against the countertop, and his knee goes between my legs and pushes them apart. His hands run up my arms, and he cups my breasts in both hands. His rough handling continues as he gropes my tits hard, my nipples stiffening further under his touch.

Daniel lets his hands roam down over my stomach. He pulls at the waistband of my pyjama bottoms and sinks his hand into them. His fingers find my pussy wet and needy.

"Getting off on this, my little whore?" he breathes against my ear. I gasp as he sinks his fingers into my slickness. "Oh, fuck. So wet, but for who, sweetheart? Me or *him?*" He sinks his fingers deep inside me.

My lungs betray me and a long, low sigh spills from my lips. Daniel's fingers pick up the pace. I can feel an orgasm already starting. The tension is building in my lower stomach. I know Daniel knows this; he can always read my body's reaction to him.

And just like that, his fingers disappear. I pant in need and frustration and then realise what he's doing. His hands and my PJ bottoms skim my hips and the latter slip down to my ankles. Dan moves back slightly and I hear the zip of his jeans. Seconds later, he's back against me, his bare, hard cock pushing between my legs. I feel him in my wet pussy. I feel his hand reaching between my legs, and a moment later, he's inside me.

He grabs my hips and begins thrusting mercilessly into me. "Mine," he growls as he pounds my soaked cunt. "My. Fucking. Cunt," he clarifies, with a thrust to emphasise every word.

Possession. Christ, that turns me on even more. My orgasm approaches fast. Daniel's need to possess my body, to be angry and frustrated, and to have that boiling over into lust. I need it. Before I realise it, an earth-shattering climax slams into me as Daniel does.

As I ride out the crescendo of my pleasure, Daniel's own climax looms. His thrusts become more staccato and a lone moan bubbles out of him. His fingernails bite into my hips as he holds tight and makes sure he fills me with his cum.

He says nothing for a few moments, then sighs, sliding out of me, releasing his hold and tucking himself back into his jeans.

"I'm going to sleep in the spare room," he announces and slowly stumbles silently upstairs.

I'm frozen to the spot, my lower half exposed, my hands still pressed against the countertop. My moment of bliss is gone. I feel the loss of my husband in more ways than one. Tears spill over my cheeks. I wipe my face, pull up my bottoms, and make my way to bed alone.

Chapter Three

"He just left?" Fi half whispers across the meeting room table.

"Yes." I sigh.

"And he actually slept in the spare room after that?"

I roll my eyes. "Yes, and he was gone when I got up this morning." My life is a fucking mess, but at least it's keeping Fiona entertained. She reads the expression on my face too well.

"Sorry, chick. I don't mean anything by it. It's just, well...." She stumbles, looking for the right words.

"It's fucking bizarre," I say.

Fiona nods in agreement. "Well, yeah."

I groan and close the file in front of me. I slump back in the chair and look at the ceiling.

"This is so fucked up!" I lament to the heavens. And just like that, Judgy Bitch takes that as her cue to start on her latest tirade. 'If I'd just kept my legs closed', and being 'the mastermind of my own demise'. God, is this really what it is? My demise?

"What are you going to do?" Fiona asks. I feel like I'm

about to burst into tears. Again. Just then, my phone buzzes. I glance at the screen, and when I see his name, despite everything, I can't help but smile.

You okay?

Fiona stares at me. "If you dare give that man up!"

I smirk and pick up my phone to reply.

I am now.

"You really think I should pick Noah over Daniel?" I ask.

She nods and gathers up her paperwork as my phone starts to ring. "Honestly, Gem? You've been more pleasant to work for since Noah got back in touch with you. Think about it." And with that, she leaves the room, allowing me to answer my phone, and Noah's call.

His personal assistant shows me into his office after a swift knock on the door. As soon as his eyes land on me, Noah stands, rounds the table, and dismisses his assistant. By the time the door shuts with a thud, he's on me. His mouth crushes against mine, his hands cupping my face.

I drink in his heat, his attention, and the tenderness with which it's delivered. It's only been a day, but, God, I've missed this man.

Fiona's words echo in my mind and I try to let the reality of them sink in as Noah's mere presence acts like a balm on my very soul.

"Are you sure you're okay?" Noah asks, still cupping my face, his forehead resting against mine.

I let out a long, slow breath. "I'm as okay as I can be in the circumstances."

He nods, drops his hands to mine, and pulls me to the

large leather sofa in the corner of the room where lunch is set out for us on the coffee table.

When I have myself finally settled on the chair, I can feel Noah's eyes on me. "Are you going to tell me what it is now?" He stares, grabbing a grape without looking, and popping it in his mouth.

"What?"

His forehead creases and his eyebrows threaten to meet. It's just not fair that this man can read me so well.

"Daniel, I take it?"

I wince. I know what he's reading from me, but I'm not sure this is a conversation I want to have with him. This whole situation has me hurting enough people already, without adding in more.

"Did he hurt you, Gem?"

What the fuck? "Jesus Christ. No! Where would you get an idea like that? You really think I would be with someone capable of that?"

He puts his hand on my knee and I pause to take a deep breath.

Cheating on the one you're cheating with. Judgy Bitch laughs. *How's that working for you?* God, I hate her, but she has a point. That *is* what this feels like and, until now, it hadn't. Noah's thumb traces absently over my knee, and he waits.

"Dan's reaction when he came home last night just wasn't what I expected, that's all." I attempt to explain. "But, he was drunk... So..." The words fail me. I can't bring myself to say them.

Noah knows. I can see it written all over his face. "You slept with him?"

I shake my head. "No, it's not like that. Yes, there was sex, but it's not what you think. It was angry. It was just dirty fucking. We didn't fuck... he fucked." I run my hands through my hair. "Christ, I'm not explaining this right. He was drunk. He came in, he called me names, he asked who was bigger, who was better. He called me more names, and I went to slap him, so he grabbed my wrists. He was so turned on, Noah."

Noah removes his hand from my leg and sits back, digesting what I'm saying. He subtly shakes his head, dismissing whatever thought flashed through his mind. I tuck my hair behind my ear and my neck is exposed. I clasp my hand over it when I see Noah's eyes widen and I realise my mistake.

"Jesus Christ, you have a hickie?" He yanks my hand from my neck to make sure he wasn't seeing things. "He marked you and hate fucked you?"

I grimace. Fuck, that makes it sound so bad. "Yes."

"Where?"

"Where, what?"

"Where did he...? In your bedroom?"

"The kitchen. I wasn't allowed to touch him or speak, and then he turned me around, my hands on the kitchen counter, and he fucked me. When he was done, he just fucked off to the spare room. Are you pissed?"

Noah smirks. "A little. I'm also a lot jealous, and..." He grabs my hand and presses it to his groin, "...a lot turned on by it." I feel his cock, hard and thick, beneath my hand. "What names did he call you?"

I look away, embarrassed. "He called me a cheating whore and asked me if you left my cunt feeling well fucked after." Another smirk and a lurch of his dick in my hand.

"Get over here," he growls and pulls my other wrist, making me move until I have no option but to straddle his lap. "Let me tell you something, Gemma Elliott. I may get pissed off, I may get jealous, but I accept those feelings as part of being with a married woman. While I don't like the idea of Daniel's cock in *my* pussy, he's your husband, and I accept it. But it would seem as though your dear husband feels the same."

I try to protest, but the facts support what Noah is suggesting. I'm not allowed to think about it further. Noah drags me back to the situation at hand with a roll of his hips, and all I can think of is how great my need is to have him inside me again.

He knows it too, because I moan when he asks, "And do I leave my girl's pretty little pussy feeling well fucked when I'm done?"

I roll my hips against him. "I don't know." I smirk. "Ask me afterwards." I lean in, pressing my lips against his, and let him envelop me.

Chapter Four

Days pass since that night in almost nothing but silence. Daniel is still sleeping in the spare room. It's at the point where I'm starting to convince myself that he was so drunk he doesn't even remember it happening.

He appears in the living room doorway, leaning casually against the frame. "I think we need to talk, Gem." *Time to reap what you sow*, Judgy Bitch pipes up.

"Okay," I croak out.

"I've been thinking, a *lot*, about everything since I found out," he starts. "I'm utterly devastated that after seventeen years of marriage, you would do this to me."

I can't bear it. I don't think I can sit here and listen to this long and torturous list of reasons as to why I'm a bitch and how he just can't live with me anymore. "Look, if you want a divorce I get it. Just tell me, Daniel!" I blurt out.

Daniel's face falls more. Jesus, I didn't think that was even possible. He walks to the sofa opposite me and sits down. "But that's the problem, Gemma. I don't want a divorce. I don't want to lose my wife."

Oh, God. He's going to ask me to choose. I can't! Tears prickle my eyes. "I don't understand," I mumble.

"I don't want a divorce. I want my wife. I want it like it was before." He looks at me, searches my face for something, and seems to find it. "You really love him, don't you?" he asks, and the tears roll down my cheeks, seeming to give him the only answer he needs. "I don't know how to handle it, Gem." His voice is laced with what almost sounds like a plea. I can find no words, and he continues, "I love you. I want you to stay. But I'm so angry with what you've done. I'm jealous that someone else has touched you, but that also turns me on."

Noah's similar words from days ago echo through my head.

"I'm hurt and angry, but when I think about it, all I can think about is how it makes me want to fuck you. It's fucked up, Gem. Who reacts that way to their wife cheating on them?"

He's right; it's not the most common reaction to a cheating spouse.

"I don't know what to say, Daniel. I do love you both. I wish I could just pick and straighten out this whole mess, but it's impossible. And yes, I know how much of a heartless bitch that makes me." I stare at the floor. I can't look him in the eye after telling him again that I also love Noah.

"Doesn't he get jealous that you fuck me, or doesn't he care?" Daniel asks out of nowhere.

I look up at him, taken aback by his question. "He gets jealous. He hates the thought of you and me together... but it turns him on too."

"I'm so pissed off at the thought of him touching you that I want to fuck you. I want to fill up that pretty pussy of yours until you can think of only me, until it's my name you're screaming out as you come for me." A perfect mix of lust and anger shimmers across his features. "Does the thought of that turn you on, Gemma?"

I blush. I feel the heat flooding my cheeks just as it's already been flooding my cunt up to this point. "Yes," I admit, licking my lips, my mouth suddenly dry.

Daniel leans back, undoes his jeans, and lets his cock spring free. "Then get yourself over here and take me in your mouth. Show me what a good little wife you can be." His hand reaches behind my neck and encourages my face to his lap.

I move quickly, getting to my knees between his legs, my hands on his thighs, waiting for him to tell me again not to touch him. Instead, he just stares at me, lets his hand knot in a fistful of my hair, and pushes his cock into my waiting mouth.

"Oh, fuck!" He hisses, his eyes closing, his head falling back in delight as I run my tongue over the length of his cock and sink completely over his hard dick.

Daniel's hand helps me find the perfect rhythm of thrusts with his grip on my hair. His head drops forward as he watches every move I make with such intensity I think it might just make me burst into flames.

My eyes never leave his the entire time I have him in my mouth. He pushes himself deeper, and I can see that he's looking at me, trying to judge how far he'll get away with pushing me. I gag, my eyes start to water, but I can't give up the intensity I feel as he stares at me. I am a whore. I am a cock hungry slut. I am so incredibly turned on by the look he's giving me, the fire in his eyes, the need, the desire, and even the anger. I want it all. Some part of me needs to be burned by the rawness of it all.

I moan as Daniel's unyielding stare drives me on, and

I'm rewarded with a pulsing in his cock and a slow blinking sigh from my husband. He's so close now, and all I want to do is please him, feel him exploding down my throat, and lick him clean.

Daniel's glare intensifies, and just at the moment when he loses control and his pleasure erupts from him, he pulls out of my mouth, yanking me off him by the hair as he comes over my face, neck, and hair. "You haven't earned my spunk yet," he rasps at me after the last ribbons of hot cum splash across my face.

I sit there, my mouth open, stunned at what just happened. Surprised by just how much more turned on it makes me to be used like that. Shocked that after what I thought was a turning point in the conversation, I'm back to feeling like the filthy whore being punished and taught a lesson. It gets me off to think about it in those terms. It shouldn't, but, by God, it does.

He lifts his leg over me and shuffles off the sofa, tucking himself back into his jeans and walking out of the room. Leaving me sitting there with the proverbial egg on my face. Frustrated, used, and desperate.

Chapter Five

I feel adrift in a sea of mixed signals, fucked up emotions, guilt, and the hottest sex of my life. When I'm with Noah, I feel guilty, I feel turned on, I feel loved. When I'm with Daniel, I feel guilty, I feel used, but I still feel turned on and loved. I flit from one to the other like a hummingbird between flowers, but this is starting to feel worse than the secrets and lies before Daniel knew what was happening.

Judgy Bitch's daily tirade on what I am, how I brought this on myself, how I'm just a greedy trollop, makes me feel about an inch tall. Something has to give. Something has to be changed because if I keep doing this back and forth between the two men I love, I'm going to come apart at the seams.

* * *

"This is really getting to you, Gemma," Noah states as he studies me, a faraway look surely on my face.

"I'm fine." I fake a smile.

There's almost a growl from him and he stares at me

intently. "Don't lie to me. I know you. I know that face." I glance at him. "That's the face my girl has when she's coming up with a decision after weighing up all the possible scenarios. Are you done with...?" Noah's voice trails off and his index finger makes a back-and-forth gesture between us.

"No," I say without a moment of hesitation. While I have no idea what the fuck to do or where to take this, doing anything without Noah isn't the answer.

"You don't like this back and forth, do you?" he asks with a perception I didn't even know was possible. I smile a little, and he looks at me in confusion. "What?"

"I really didn't know that you knew me that well," I explain. "Daniel wouldn't..." My words are cut off with Noah's mouth on mine. He's telling me he doesn't want to be compared. It seems I know him just as well as he knows me.

When the kiss ends, Noah looks at me with a gaze that makes me fear what he's about to say. "Where is Daniel right now?"

I stare at him. "Why?"

"Gem, where is he?"

"He's at home."

"Call him and get him to come here."

I shake my head. There is nothing about that idea that is even remotely sensible. "No! Jesus! Noah, what can that possibly achieve? That's not a good idea!"

Noah remains adamant that this is exactly what I need to do. Judgy Bitch is howling with laughter and taunting me about how my life is about to go down in flames. "Gem, he knows you're with me. He knows what we do. How will it hurt to have him over here?"

I stare at him in a state of shock. Has he lost his ever-loving mind? I shiver. "Are you crazy? What do I say if he asks why?"

"Tell him that we all need to talk. I'll talk to him if I fucking need to, Gemma. Now call him."

I lift my phone from my bag, admitting defeat. "Hey, it's me," I reply when he answers. "Listen, I, um…" I hesitate. Noah looks at me and waits. "I'm at Noah's, and… and you need to come over, because, we, I mean, I think we all need to talk about this." I wait for what Daniel is going to say. I expect the worst.

"I'll be right over," he replies.

"Oh." I'm stunned that he just agreed to meet up with Noah again. "Uh, see you soon then," I tell him and hang up the phone. I look at Noah and shake my head. "I don't know what the fuck you think is going to happen, but this is a very bad idea. As long as you know that."

Noah nods and kisses my forehead. "And you need to trust me."

I do, though. I trust him implicitly. That doesn't mean I don't think he's lost all leave of his senses. We sit, nervously waiting for Daniel to arrive.

Chapter Six

Noah holds the door open for Dan to enter. "Thanks for coming over," he tells him. Daniel gives him a cold look and I already want the ground to open up and swallow me. I love both of these men, but this pulling from one to the other is killing me.

"What's this about?" Daniel asks him, practically ignoring me.

"It's about Gemma. We're pulling her in two different directions, and it's not going to be good for either of us in the long run."

I can see my husband thinking about what my lover is saying.

Daniel nods. "I agree. She's miserable like this." Noah nods too. "But what do we do? Pick for her?"

Noah frowns and then glances over at me. "Gem, can you go and make me and Daniel a coffee? I need a little man-to-man chat with him."

Now I know he's lost his mind. I look at him and then at Daniel with my mouth hanging open, knowing that by the end of this conversation, I'll be calling an ambulance for both of them.

Daniel looks at me and smiles, attempting to reassure me. "It's fine. Honestly, you're not happy like this. I can at least hear him out."

I'm lost, Judgy Bitch is scarily silent, and I feel sure that I must have slipped through a crack in the fabric of time and into a parallel universe. There's nothing else that can explain this. I nod absently and walk to the kitchen while Noah and Daniel disappear into the living room and close the door.

* * *

With two coffee cups in hand, I make my way back to the living room. I pause. *Should I knock?* I listen and don't hear any raised voices. My heartbeat quickens, and I push the handle down with my elbow and shove the door with my backside, catching the tail end of the conversation between my men.

"I agree. I'll follow your lead," Daniel says.

Both men clam up the second they're aware I'm here. I stand in the doorway and stare at them, first Daniel, unharmed, and then Noah, also unharmed, with a mild smirk on his face. I hand them each a cup in turn.

"Thanks," they both chime at once.

I wait and watch as they sip at their coffees until I just can't take it anymore. "Is one of you going to tell me what the fuck is going on?"

Noah shrugs. "We just came to an arrangement."

I stare at him.

"An agreement more than anything," Daniel says.

I stare at him too.

Noah sets his cup on the coffee table. "Honestly, it's okay," he tells me, his hands going to my waist and pulling me against him slightly.

Daniel stands beside us, and I fear it's about to kick off. His coffee cup joins Noah's on the table, and his hands go around my waist too, pulling me against his other side.

"Have I passed out and bumped my head?" I ask in utter disbelief.

Noah smiles and leans in to kiss my neck. "Not that I noticed."

Daniel leans in and kisses me on the opposite side. "You seem perfectly healthy to me."

"Oh, Jesus." I moan between them. "Is this what you thought was a good solution?" Two mouths are on my neck and shoulders, and four hands hold me between them.

"Now you don't have to pick between us," Daniel murmurs as his hand reaches for my right breast.

"Now you can have us both, at the same time," Noah purrs against my throat, his hand reaching my left breast.

"Christ," is all I can manage before I turn my face to Daniel and catch his mouth, enjoying the feeling of two sets of hot hands. They are both feeling my arse and my tits, pulling me against them, enclosing me between them like the filling in some exquisite man sandwich.

I moan and turn from Daniel to Noah, capturing his mouth, kissing him. Noah's hands reach for the buttons on my blouse, he undoes them, and his hands and Daniel's find my bare skin.

Daniel works on the zip at the back of my skirt. It falls to the floor, and Noah uses the opportunity to peel my blouse from my shoulders and cast it aside. I stand between them in just my lacy underwear and stockings.

My husband presses his hard cock against my arse, and

my lover presses his hard cock against my lower stomach. I feel like such a slut, but it's turning me on so much.

Noah kisses me hard, his hands over my breasts. Daniel undoes my bra, and Noah finishes taking it off me. Daniel's lips touch the back of my neck and he sinks lower, kissing a trail down until he reaches the small of my back. His hands go for the waistband on my knickers, and he slides them down my hips and legs.

My lover's hand glides over my stomach, his fingers sliding between my soaked labia and finding my clit. My husband's hands grab my arse, and his tongue slips between my buttocks. I put one arm around Noah's neck to keep me upright, and the other hand reaches for Dan's head. My head falls back and a long moan escapes me as I come between them both for the first time.

When I come back to my senses, both men are grinning, pleased with their handiwork, pleased at the sight of me already undone and naked between them.

Noah's thumb grazes my bottom lip. "Fuck, you have the sexiest mouth." He steps back from me. His hands sink to the zipper on his jeans and he looks at me, all the while undoing his jeans and freeing his cock from his underwear.

I can't help but stare when I see his rock-hard cock spring free, overwhelmed with the need to have it in my mouth and feast on him like I've been starved. Dan lifts his head from my asshole and takes in what's happening in front of him. I'm sure his curiosity is piqued by what Noah has on display. He soon understands exactly what's happening and pushes my legs further apart. His fingers find my clit and pussy, and his tongue returns to my arsehole.

Noah moves in against me and kisses me hard, his fingers knotting in my hair, and then moves back. Daniel's positioning of me has me in the perfect stance for bending under Noah's guiding hand and lowering my mouth towards his flagrant erection, now just inches from my face.

I don't need any encouragement to take my lover's cock into my mouth, enveloping him in the wet warmth my tongue has to offer. My husband is working me into a frenzy from behind, his tongue fucking my ass, and his fingers offering the same service to my soaked sex. He has me ready to come again, and soon.

Noah pushes forward and hits the back of my throat. I gag, and I can feel my pussy pulse with my impending climax. Dan knows, and his fingers and tongue disappear. I'm vaguely aware of him standing behind me. Then I feel it; his cock is replacing his fingers. He holds my hips and slides inside me.

Sweet Christ, I'm being spit roasted. That thought alone is enough to send me crashing over the edge as I come hard, flooding Daniel's cock with my juices and moaning loudly around Noah's cock in my mouth.

He hisses. "Fuck, that feels so good when you make those delicious noises vibrate through my dick."

Daniel's thumb presses against my arsehole, and just as I'm starting to ride out the orgasm I've just had, he slides it inside me as he thrusts forcefully into my drenched cunt. Another climax shakes through me, and I gag on my lover's cock as he begins to wantonly fuck my face.

Judgy Bitch is quiet and watching from the corner of my mind. I feel so incredibly sexy to be so gloriously filled between these two beautiful men in such a decadent and utterly erotic way. My lover and my husband enjoying my body, indulging in me together, until, finally, all three of us come.

Noah shoots his hot cum right down my throat, and like

a greedy whore, I drink it all down. Daniel grabs my hips and slams into me hard as he unloads everything he has deep inside me. I come apart between them, overloaded with the deliciousness of feeling so slutty, full of cum, and totally spent. We all collapse onto the sofa soon after, and I know that things will never be the same again.

Chapter Seven

E ventually, we made it up to Noah's bedroom, and I'm pretty sure the entire neighbourhood is now aware of what is going on in Noah's house with how loudly both men had me coming. I'm lying here between the two men who have my heart and have just had my body, sweat glistening over all three of us. Judgy Bitch is rocking in the corner. She didn't see this outcome coming any more than I did.

"Are you okay?" Noah murmurs against my back.

"Uh-huh." I sigh, still not recovered from the orgasm that has just rocked my world.

"We haven't worn you out yet, have we?" Daniel asks in front of me.

I lick my lips and try to focus on him properly, shaking my head a little as I reply, "No. Not yet."

Noah's lips hit my shoulder with a soft growl. "Not yet? That sounds like a challenge to me, Daniel," he says against my skin, staring at my husband.

"I like a challenge." Daniel dips his head to my tits and sucks a nipple into his mouth.

"Oh, Christ. Are you trying to kill me?" I breathlessly ask, my hand already in my husband's hair.

A low, appreciative agreement vibrates through Daniel's mouth and my tit.

"What a way to go," my lover agrees, and his lips find my neck.

Death by orgasm. I'm sure it's possible, and I'm sure it's about to happen to me. Both men feast on what they can reach. Daniel has my breasts and pussy at his mouth and fingers. Noah has my neck, shoulders, and arse.

I gasp when I feel Daniel's fingers sliding inside me, but this time, I'm greedy for more. Since we made it to the bedroom and all three of us removed our clothing, both men, my men, have been teasing the orgasms from me with their hands and mouths, but now I want more.

"Oh, fuck!" I moan as Noah's fingertips touch my arsehole, and I need to press myself against his fingers, seeking more.

"Something you need, Gemma?" he asks, and I can hear the smirk he's wearing without even seeing it.

"Tell us," Daniel encourages.

I moan again and grind against both hands, desperate to take both men inside me, needy to feel stretched out by both of their cocks at the same time. "Oh, God. I want you inside me," I moan. "Both of you."

At my utterance, Daniel rubs his thumb over my clit and I feel like it burns right through to my core.

"Are you wet enough to take us both?" Noah asks, his fingers suddenly joining Daniel's in my pussy.

I come. The subtle encouragement from both mixed with the extra stimulation of both of them naked and pressed against either side of me just takes me over. I can't remember ever being this turned on, or this wet, or this needy.

"Oh, fuck yes, Gemma. You're soaked. Give me that sweet pussy juice so I can take your arse," my lover purrs in my ear as I start to recover my senses. His hand is working itself from my cunt to my ass, sweeping the wetness backwards and coating my other opening with the necessary lubricant.

"God, you really love being the whore, don't you, Mrs Elliott?" my husband taunts. My body involuntarily reacts; I can't help myself.

"Fuck, Daniel! You made her even wetter!" Noah breathes as he works his fingers over my holes.

"That's because she's a good little cock slut, hungry to take us both," Daniel murmurs against my lips, kissing me hard once his declaration is made. He's right. I am. The more they tease me, the more they call me names and congratulate each other on how horny they're making me, the worse my desperation to have them both at once becomes.

Noah's hand disappears for a second and his cock replaces it. Daniel's tongue duels with mine, and his fingers slip forward to my clit. Noah's cock slips between my wet labia and sinks into my pussy, a low moan rumbling through his chest.

"Fuck, you feel incredible." He groans, pushing deep into my pussy. "That's it, Gem. Soak my cock with your cunt. Get me nice and wet to slide into your arse." His words and both their actions send me over again.

"Fuck!" he exclaims as he feels my pussy constrict around his cock, bearing down on him in my climax. Daniel's mouth goes back to my nipples, and another loud groan rips through me.

Noah's cock slides from my cunt, and I feel it against my arse. I open my eyes, Daniel's find mine, and he grins at me, my breast still enveloped by his mouth.

My lover's cock presses against my arsehole, demanding entry, and I can't help but push myself back on him. I'm hungry now to have him inside me. I need it too much to think straight.

"Easy!" Noah hisses behind me, a hand on my hip to attempt to still me. I know he needs me to slow. I know he wants to make sure he's not hurting me in any way and to keep his own control. But it's just not enough and not quickly enough. I can feel my arsehole on the breach of giving in and letting him inside me, and I need it. I press against him, fighting his resistance on my hip, and groan loudly when he finally gets in past that ring of muscle attempting to keep him out.

His mouth is back on my shoulder, and he nips softly on my skin. I want him to mark me. I want them both to mark me and claim me as theirs. I belong to both of them, heart and soul.

Daniel watches as my eyes roll back in my head as Noah's cock sinks into my ass completely. "Oh, fuck, you're hot with a cock in your arse. Your face is perfect." He kisses me softly, his tongue tempting my mouth gently. His hand between my legs pushes against my thigh, encouraging me to lift my leg over his. His body slides against me, his cock pressing through my wetness. I feel him line up with my pussy entrance, and he thrusts gently, pushing himself inside.

The arm I have against the mattress hooks around Daniel's neck, pulling him against me. The other arm reaches behind me and finds Noah's arse. I'm lying in between them, both men inside me, and it feels exquisite.

Both men are rolling their hips, thrusting inside me, timing their movements against each other so one is thrusting in as the other is pulling back to do the same. My lover's hands have my hips, holding my arse for him to claim with every stroke, every thrust. My husband's hands have my thigh and face, both men giving me everything they have. Both men making love to the woman they have loved for years. I melt against them both. This is where I was meant to be. This is what heaven feels like, and I never want it to end.

Chapter Eight

Six months later

"Where are we going?" I ask Daniel as he drives us down the street in a leafy suburb not far from where we live now.

"You'll see." He grins, before indicating and pulling into a driveway.

I shake my head and look at the house we're now sitting outside. It's huge. I look too at the other car already in the driveway; Noah's. "What are you up to?" I ask him, glancing over as he gets out of the car.

"I told you." He smiles. "You'll see."

The front door of the house opens and Noah is standing there, smiling. "Come on then!" he calls to me, beckoning me out of the car.

I'm curious as hell to see what my two men are up to this time. The last three months have been a rollercoaster ride. Sometimes, I'm with Daniel alone. Sometimes, I'm with Noah alone. Most of the time, I'm with them both in some sort of weird polyamorous relationship that I would never have previously thought possible.

Noah and Daniel, lover and husband, seem to have forged this bizarre friendship out of a mutual appreciation of me. It's not totally without its issues, but those seem to be worked out in lust, both men utterly determined to keep claiming me back from the other by burying their cocks inside me and emptying their balls into me.

I get out of the car and head towards the house behind Daniel, Noah grinning like the cat that got the cream. My husband takes my left hand, my lover takes my right, and between them, they guide me around the large, empty period house with its five bedrooms and three bathrooms; one family, and two en suite.

The house is gorgeous; it's like every fairytale home I dreamed of as a child. It's just like the ones I talked about to both of them back when we were young, foolish, and didn't know what a house like this really cost. When we make it back to the large family room, both men look at me expectantly.

"Well?" Noah asks.

"Well, what?" I ask.

"Do you like it?" Daniel prompts.

I consider my answer. "It's a gorgeous house. You know it's the kind of place I've always imagined living in, but I still don't understand."

Noah and Daniel exchange a look between them; a small victory I'm apparently unaware of has occurred.

"It's for us," Noah tells me.

"Us?" I echo.

"We thought it would suit us." Daniel attempts to clarify. "*All* of us."

Sanity has clearly left my husband and lover. I look at them both in utter disbelief.

"You want all of us to live together?" I ask.

They nod.

"Like, you BOTH want to own this?"

Again, they nod.

Well, fuck me, Judgy Bitch says. *Finally*, I think, *she and I agree on something*. "We're all going to live here?" I ask, still not believing what I'm hearing. "All three of us together?"

The husband and lover tag team nods again. I look around the room and think about the house that lies beyond. *Holy shit.*

"Gem, are you okay? You look a little pale," Daniel tells me. My knees feel weak and my body feels like lead. Their expressions change as they watch me sink to the floor before them. Everything in slow motion. Their smiles disappear, they start moving towards me, and blackness enshrouds me.

Chapter Nine

"Honestly, I'm fine. You didn't need to bring me to A&E," I grumble, embarrassed at my extreme reaction to their announcement. I can feel the fire in my cheeks as they stand, one on either side of me, both of my hands held by them.

A doctor appears around the curtain and glances over the situation he finds in front of him. "Uh, Mrs Elliott?" he asks. I nod. "We, uh, usually only allow family members in the cubicle." He looks from Daniel to Noah and back to me.

"I'm her boyfriend," Noah pipes up.

"I'm her husband," Daniel adds. "And we are a family."

I can feel the burn of my cheeks sink down my neck and over my chest.

"Uh, uh huh, okay. Well, uh, the good news is that your blood work has all come back clear, Mrs Elliott. Everything looks good and perfectly clear."

"Then why did she faint?" Noah asks, squeezing my hand a little more.

"Well, sir, it's pretty common for someone in Mrs Elliot's condition."

WHAT? The doctor reads the room well, giving me a sheepish look that he might just have dropped a bombshell. "Did you know you're pregnant?" he asks. The tension between us all is palpable.

I shake my head.

"Ah, well, congratulations, Mrs Elliott. I'll give you a letter for your GP, and he can sort you out with your first antenatal appointment."

I nod. I'm mute. The power of speech has left me. It's left my men too, apparently, their white faces and blank expressions a mirror of my own reaction. The doctor nods to all three of us and hastily makes his retreat from the cubicle.

The only one not speechless at the news is Judgy Bitch. She's back to normal and crowing one blindingly obvious problem. *Whose baby is it?* And I know what Judgy Bitch already thinks. I've been with Daniel for years and it never happened. Now, Noah is on the scene, and I'm pregnant. I'll admit she's got a point.

I watch the faces of my husband and lover, looking for some sort of reaction to the information that has just been dumped into all of our laps. Noah looks at me, and then at Daniel. Daniel does the same. I watch in silence as both men reach out a hand and place it on my still somersaulting stomach, smiling.

My husband looks at my lover. "We're going to be dads!" He grins.

Noah has a dazed grin on his face. "We're going to have a baby?" he says, still smiling in disbelief. The sweet surprise coming off both men in waves is contagious.

I nod at Noah with a smile. "Apparently so."

Daniel takes my hand and gives it a squeeze. "It's going to be okay," he tells me. "I promise."

Noah leans over and kisses my cheek. "We... all three of

us... well, I mean, four of us now.... We'll be a great little family!"

My husband extends his hand out to my lover. Both men shake hands heartily. "Congratulations." Daniel grins at Noah.

Noah sighs with a smile. "And you, mate. Fucking hell, we timed buying that house well."

My ears process what I've just heard. "Wait!" I say, grabbing Noah and Daniel's arms. "You already *bought* the house?"

My husband nods. "Well, we knew that if you thought about it for too long you would decide against it or something, so we conspired for the last two months, and the house was finally ours this morning. Noah went and collected the keys."

I stare at them both in disbelief. *Sneaky bastards.* I'm going to have to watch these two. A nurse sticks her head around the curtain and enters to hand me over a letter for my doctor.

"Here you go, love." She smiles, handing it over. "Doc says that's you free to leave. Here's a prescription for some folic acid, and just make sure you get to see your GP." She nods to both men and leaves just as quickly as she arrived.

Daniel holds my hand. "Ready to go?"

I nod.

Noah smiles and both men help me up off the hospital trolley. They take it in turns to kiss me softly. I need to say it. It's already burning into my brain and tying my stomach in knots.

"Guys, do you want to know? I mean..." I rub my hand absently over my not-even-there-yet bump, "...you can't both be the biological father."

Noah's finger appears over my lips.

"Don't even say that," Daniel answers.

"*WE* are the daddies," Noah agrees.

"You don't want to know?" I ask again.

"Nope."

"Never," they reply together.

I shake my head in incredulity. These two men have my heart, and they never cease to amaze me. I smile at them. "I love you both so much."

"We love you too," they reply, and with one of my men on each side of me, I head out of the hospital, ready for the unexpected.

Epilogue

Their hands wrap around my naked form. Four hands holding onto me, on my breasts, my arse, my baby bump. Daniel's hands tease my breasts and rub gently over my swollen stomach.

Noah's hands grab my ass and cup my face as he kisses me deeply. "Fuck, you're glorious when you're pregnant," he whispers against my lips.

"Mmmm," agrees Daniel from behind me. "Might just have to keep you bare and knocked up." He chuckles with a kiss on my shoulder.

The door of our bedroom swings open, making all three of us jump. Daniel pulls the covers high over us all.

"Mummy! Daddies!" comes the cry as a tiny person flings himself up onto the bed. Daniel grabs our son before he can bounce on me and my growing belly.

"Daddy Dan, I had a bad dream." Our boy weeps.

"Aww, little man. What happened?" Noah asks him.

"I got a sister." He cries against Daniel's chest. Noah grins, and his hand rests gently on my belly as I giggle, unseen by our son.

* * *

When I met Noah again in that hotel six years ago, I would never have predicted that I would end up here, between the two men I love with all my heart, living together as one big happy family. We have never found out who Oscar's biological father is. Some days, he is the spitting image of Noah, and other days, the sparkle in his eyes and the sound of his laugh make him a carbon copy of Daniel. He is a very lucky little boy with three parents who adore him completely. In two months, we will welcome another little person into our family. I haven't told anyone, but I already know that poor Oscar's nightmare is becoming a reality; he's getting a sister. But if Dan and Noah can grow to accept each other, and even turn into family, then I'm sure our son will be able to cope with having a baby sister. Fate definitely has a sense of humour.

* * *

Enjoy this? Why not read the next in the series -
Unexpected

He's my best friend's dad. I wasn't supposed to see him like that, but I wanted him, and nothing was going to stop me until I got him.

She's my daughter's best friend. The last person I should have been interested in. But here I am, addicted to how good she feels beneath me, ready to give her anything she wants.

It wasn't to be anything more than a fling. An affair. Two people who just wanted to be with each other in the heat of the moment.

Until something else took over. Until it was more. Until it became something to tear their world apart. Can love conquer all? Or was this just lust taken too far?

About the Author

Dee Lish is an Irish author who loves to indulge her imagination with some filthy stories. She's been publishing under other pen names since 2014, but in 2023 returned to her erotic roots.

She likes to spend what little spare time she has binge watching her favourite shows, reading, and making messes and memories with her two children.

You can follow her on social media, or join her newsletter for all the latest naughtiness!

Also by Dee Lish

Succumb to Me Series

The Mistress

The Ponygirl

The Handled

The Punished

The Corrupted

The Student

One Handed Reads Series

Teased

Owned

Seduced

Tempted

Desired

Unexpected

* * *

Dee Lish also writes romance as Leighann Duncan

www.authorleighannduncan.co.uk

www.ingramcontent.com/pod-product-compliance
Lightning Source LLC
Chambersburg PA
CBHW030811190726
48285CB00003B/1134